W9-BHU-839

BRAND SPANKING NEW!

DOUG's™
Vampire Caper

Created by Jim Jinkins

Adapted by
Nancy E. Krulik

Illustrated by
Pete List and Cheng-li Chan, Tony
Curanaj, Chris Dechert, Brian Donnelly,
Ray Feldman, Chris Palesty, Matt
Peters, and Jonathan Royce

JUMBO
PICTURES
INC.

GRADE A QUALITY

DISNEP
PRESS

New York

Original Script by Joe Fallon

Original Characters for "The Funnies"
Developed by Jim Jinkins and Joe Aaron

SPECIAL EDITION

Printed in the United States of America.

The text for this book is set in 16-point Berkeley Book.

Library of Congress Catalog Card Number: 97-65661

ISBN: 0-7868-4240-7

DOUG's™

Vampire Caper

Chapter 1

"Someone in this school is the Bat Master, vampire leader of the bats," Connie Benge declared.

The group of kids gathered outside Beebe Bluff Middle School started to shake. It was almost Halloween and everybody was thinking about scary stuff. Connie's comments made everyone extra nervous.

Could this be true? Could there be a vampire among them?

The whole thing seemed kind of weird to Doug Funnie. Doug had known these kids a long time. He'd taken classes with them. He'd even eaten at Swirly's with them. And not one of them had ever ordered a blood-flavored milk shake! They *couldn't* be vampires.

Besides, Connie really couldn't be trusted. Connie's new hobby was spreading rumors.

Still, there *were* a lot of spooky Halloween decorations hanging around the school this year. Some of them were really creepy—especially those real live bats hanging in the bell tower.

"Bats gather like that to seek their master," Connie said knowingly as she pointed to the bats in the tower. "You know what that means."

The kids all stared blankly at Connie. They had no idea what that meant.

Connie sighed. Hadn't she just told them? "It means someone in this school is the Bat Master!"

"I bet Mr. Heaver is the vampire," Ned suggested.

"Which Mr. Heaver?" Doug asked. There were two Mr. Heavers at Beebe Bluff Middle School. Homer Heaver was the wood shop teacher. His brother, Road Heaver, taught metal shop.

Doug thought about it. What if one of the Heavers really *was* the Bat Master? What if Doug had to stand outside the school one night, all alone? Homer Heaver could fly right up to him and turn him into a vampire!

Doug began to envision what Mr. Heaver would be like as a vampire.

"*Bleagh!*" Doug imagined Homer Heaver saying in a voice just like an actor in the old Dracula movies.

"Don't hypnotize me," Doug would beg.

But Homer Heaver would give Doug a strange look. "Who's hypnotizing?" Doug imagined Mr. Heaver asking as he ran his hands along the bark of a tree. "Just look at that wood. It's so smooth and even. An ideal building material."

No, Doug decided, Homer Heaver was not a vampire. How could he be? He was more interested in making bookshelves than biting necks!

But there *was* his brother, Road Heaver. Road Heaver was a pretty weird teacher. What if *he* were the vampire? Worse yet— what if he were a *super steel* vampire, with shimmering metal wings?

"Regular bat wings are weak!" Doug imagined Road Heaver shrieking. "I use steel! I am the vampire master of metal."

But steel would be too heavy. The Road Heaver vampire wouldn't be able to fly. Still, he might be able to rig something up.

"I'll have to add engines," Doug imagined the Road Heaver vampire saying. "A slant six on each arm!"

Doug laughed to himself. Road Heaver wasn't a vampire, either. He was just a weird shop teacher.

"I don't think either Heaver is a vampire," Doug told Connie.

Connie put her hands on her hips. She wasn't through yet. "Then what about Ms. Kristal?" she suggested. "Anything's possible with Ms. Kristal."

Doug gasped. His English teacher a vampire? Could it be possible?

Doug thought about it. He'd never actually seen Ms. Kristal smile so her teeth showed. What if Ms. Kristal's teeth were actually long, sharp fangs?

Doug imagined his English teacher sitting behind a coffin-shaped desk wearing a long black cape.

"Listen to them, the children of the

night," Ms. Kristal might say in a slight Transylvanian accent. "What music they make!" Then Ms. Kristal would reach beneath her cape and pull out . . . a copy of the novel *Dracula* by Bram Stoker. "Everybody grab your books and turn to page nineteen," she would tell them.

Doug looked at Connie and shook his head. He was sure Ms. Kristal wasn't the Bat Master. She was just a very dramatic English teacher.

But if Ms. Kristal wasn't the Bat Master, who was?

Chapter 2

Skunky pointed to Mr. Crushie, the school maintenance worker. "What about that Mr. Crushie dude?" he asked. "We don't know anything about him."

The kids looked over at Mr. Crushie. He was standing just beneath the bell tower, arguing with the school principal. The kids were shocked. They'd never seen anybody argue with Mr. White before.

Vampires are pretty gutsy creatures, Doug thought.

"It's your duty to go up there and make those bats scat!" the kids heard Mr. White order Mr. Crushie.

But Mr. Crushie didn't budge. "I can't," he said simply.

Mr. White stared angrily at Mr. Crushie. He was not used to people talking back. "Why not?" he demanded.

Connie glanced knowingly at the other kids. "He can't make them leave because *he's* the Bat Master," she whispered.

But Mr. Crushie had a different explanation. "I can't because bats make me feel all

icky." Mr. Crushie shivered and squealed, "*Eeeew!*"

Skeeter Valentine, Doug's best buddy, shook his head and said to the other kids, "I don't think it's him."

"Well, keep watching the bell tower!" Connie urged. "The Bat Master is sure to go up there to visit his loyal subjects!"

Doug shrugged. They'd just have to wait and see.

Chapter 3

The next day everyone kept their eyes on the bell tower. So far nobody had spotted the Bat Master. Still, Connie insisted he would show up—so everyone kept sneaking a peek.

As soon as school let out, Doug went outside to the back fence to meet Skeeter. But Skeeter wasn't there.

The only person standing by the fence was Skunky. He was using the fence as a drum pad. And he was playing a wild solo.

"Skunky, have you seen Skeeter?" Doug asked.

Skunky tapped his drumsticks nervously

against the fence and shook his head. "Negatori," he told Doug. Skunky clicked his sticks a little faster. Finally, he put them down and looked Doug straight in the eye.

"Doug-dude, I was thinkin'," Skunky said earnestly. "What if *I'm* the Bat Master, and I don't know it? I mean, I like my burgers rare. . . ."

"If it were you, you'd be in the tower,"

11

Doug assured him. "You heard Connie. The Bat Master will go up there to be with his subjects."

Both boys looked up at the tower, and they spotted Skeeter sitting up there among the bats.

"Hey, isn't that your bud?" Skunky asked, pointing up toward Skeeter.

So that's where Skeeter had been all this time. At first, Doug was happy to find him.

"Yeah, thanks," Doug told Skunky gratefully. "No wonder I couldn't find him. He's up in the . . ."

Doug stopped midsentence. His best friend was up in the tower—*with the bats!* That could only mean *one* thing!

Doug gulped and looked nervously at Skunky. Slowly the boys looked back up at the tower. Skeeter was gone. Skunky started to shake so hard he dropped his drumsticks.

"Sk-Skunky," Doug stammered, "did you see someone up there with the b-b-b-bats?"

"Yeah, Valentine was hangin' up there

with the bats, man," Skunky replied nervously.

Doug felt sick. His best friend was the Bat Master. He would never have believed it—*except he'd seen it with his own two eyes.*

Chapter 4

There was only one way to find out if Skeeter really was a vampire. Doug would have to find proof!

Doug went to Skeeter's house after school and pretended that he wanted to play video games. The truth was, Doug wanted to search through Skeeter's things, but to do that, he had to get Skeeter out of the room.

"You think I could have a glass of water, Skeet?" Doug asked innocently.

"Sure," Skeeter replied. "Come on."

Doug shook his head. "Let me finish this level, okay?" Doug asked.

14

Skeeter nodded and went to the kitchen. Quickly, Doug jumped up and started going through Skeeter's drawers. In the first drawer he found socks. That was pretty normal. In the next drawer he found a monkey's paw, a bloody hook, and an opera CD.

That wasn't so normal.

Doug opened the closet. That's when he saw . . . THE COFFIN . . . and a vampire day-planner!

Doug flipped open the planner. Skeeter's handwriting was pretty bad, but Doug could make out most of the words. Beebe—bit her. Chalky—bit him. Patti—bite at 11:32!

Patti! Doug's heart skipped a beat. Patti Mayonnaise was the girl of Doug's dreams. He couldn't bear the thought of Patti wandering the world seeking fresh blood.

There was no way Doug was going to let Skeeter turn Patti into a vampire!

15

Doug grabbed the vampire day-planner, burst out of Skeeter's house, and raced over to Patti's.

"Patti! Patti!" Doug called up to her open bedroom window.

Patti peeked out from behind her curtains and looked curiously at Doug. "What's wrong, Doug?" she asked sweetly.

"Skeeter's a vampire and he's going to bite you at 11:32!" Doug screamed.

Patti started to giggle. "Oh, Doug, you're so funny!" Suddenly all of the windows in Patti's house exploded open. Hundreds and hundreds of black bats flew out and soared through the air. "Skeeter bit me yesterday," Patti explained. "Today, he's scheduled to bite you!"

Quickly, Doug opened the planner. Sure enough, there it was, in bright red letters: THINGS TO DO TODAY: BITE DOUG.

Doug blushed. "Oops. I should've looked."

16

Suddenly, Doug felt someone breathing on his neck. He turned and came face-to-face with Skeeter—the Bat Master himself!

"Come on, Doug," Skeeter urged, baring his big pointy teeth. "It's fun!"

Doug tried to run. But as he turned, his path was blocked by Beebe, Chalky, and Roger. And they were all vampires!

"*AHHHH!*" Doug screamed as the gang closed in on him. He swung his arms and frantically tried to break free. But it was no use. Skeeter opened his mouth wide, and . . .

Clunk! Doug fell out of bed. It was only a nightmare.

"What a bad dream," he muttered as he pulled the covers over his head.

But just as Doug was about to drift back to sleep, he heard a familiar voice outside his window.

"Doug," Patti called up to him.

What was Patti doing at his house in the middle of the night? Doug wondered. He got out of bed and opened the curtains. He saw Patti's face in the window. Ordinarily that would have made Doug very happy. But this time Patti's face was attached to a bat's body. A Skeeter-bat flew by her side.

"Hey, Doug," the Skeeter-bat greeted him. "You wanna fly to Swirly's with us for a Swirlyicious Blood Clot Shake?"

"*AAAGGGGHHHH!*" Doug screamed. He fell out of bed with a thud. Porkchop barked.

Doug's eyes fluttered open. He looked around the room. There was no Patti-bat. And no Skeeter-bat, either.

"I hate double dreams," Doug moaned as

he climbed back in bed.

Doug didn't sleep a wink the rest of the night. He was worried about having a *triple* dream. And besides, he couldn't stop thinking about his big problem. Doug didn't know whether to tell anyone else about seeing Skeeter with the bats. After all, Skeeter was his best friend. He didn't want everybody to be afraid of him. Still, if Skeeter *was* the Bat Master, they would have a *real* reason to be afraid.

Chapter 5

Everyone at school was talking about the Bat Master. They all had different ideas about how to catch him.

"The only way to catch the Bat Master is to form teams and watch all the grown-ups," Chalky suggested. Connie nodded. That sounded good to her.

"What if it's not a grown-up?" Doug asked quietly. "What if it's one of us?" Suddenly, Doug felt someone sneak up behind him. He turned and came face-to-face with *Skeeter*. Doug gasped. Skeeter was holding a stuffed vampire decoration. The vampire had red painted blood dripping out of its mouth. It was a Halloween decoration only a vampire could love.

"Come on, guys. There's no Bat Master," Skeeter declared. "Bats of the family Desmodontidae feed on animals' blood. But there's no such thing as real vampires."

Skeeter turned and walked away down

the hall. The kids just stared after him.

"Skeeter's smart," Patti said, finally. "He must be right."

Just then Doug heard a *tap tap tap* sound coming down the hall. Skunky was walking over to meet them, and as usual he was drumming on the walls.

"Hey!" Skunky announced as he approached the group. "Doug-dude and I saw Skeeter hangin' with the bats yesterday."

"What?" Patti asked nervously.

Doug glared angrily at Skunky. *What a big mouth!* Then he looked sheepishly at Patti and nodded slowly.

Connie put her hands on her hips and glared at Doug. "Well, of course Skeeter says there's no such thing as vampires. He's covering up because *he's* the BAT MASTER!"

Everybody ran to the window and watched as Skeeter collided into a tree.

"That's one spooky hombre," Skunky remarked.

Chapter 6

Doug didn't even bother to wait for Skeeter after school. He ran straight to the library and took out some books on vampires. Then he raced up to his room and started reading. The first book was really scary. It told all about the legend of Count Dracula from Transylvania. According to the story, the count slept all day in a coffin. At night he awoke and roamed the countryside looking for fresh necks to bite. Anyone who was bitten by the count became a vampire as well.

Doug slammed the book shut. He was scared. He decided he had to talk to someone about Skeeter. He figured he'd try his dad first.

After dinner, Doug went to help his dad develop pictures in his darkroom. As they hung the negatives up to dry, Doug turned to his father. "Dad, can you tell me about preternatural phenomena?"

Doug could have sworn his father started to blush—but it was hard to tell in the red light of the darkroom. "Uh . . . uh . . . well, sure," Mr. Funnie stammered. "First a man and a woman fall in love, get married, and decide to . . ."

Doug shook his head. He didn't want to know about *that*. He wanted to know about the supernatural. "No, Dad," Doug said, "I want to know what you can tell me about *vampires*."

Mr. Funnie looked thoughtfully at his son. "Vampires, huh?" he asked.

"Yeah. Vampires." Doug replied.

"Okay," Mr. Funnie began. "First a boy vampire meets a girl vampire. They fall in love, get married, and decide to . . ."

24

Doug sighed. Obviously he was going to have to get his information from another source. But who?

The next morning Doug smelled smoke coming from his neighbor's yard. He ran outside and saw Mr. Dink operating a huge machine. Doug watched as Mr. Dink placed a big pumpkin in the machine. Then he flicked a switch. The machine hummed, then whirred, then clanked and clunked. Steam rose from the pumpkin. When the machine was finally turned off, Mr. Dink had a perfect jack-o-lantern!

Mr. Dink knew a little bit about a lot of things. Doug hoped that maybe he knew something about vampires, too.

"Hi!" Doug greeted his neighbor. "Can I ask you something?"

"Just a moment, Douglas," Mr. Dink replied. "I'm testing my new jack-o-lantern carver. Very expensive."

Mr. Dink placed another pumpkin in the carver and looked at the settings on the front of the machine. They said: EERIE, SCARY, REAL SCARY, and AHHHHHHH!

"Let's try Real Scary," Mr. Dink suggested. He moved the dial to REAL SCARY and flicked the switch. When it was finished, Mr. Dink had one real scary jack-o-lantern!

Mr. Dink seemed happy. He was ready to try another. "Now let's go for Ahhhhhhh!" he said.

Doug waited for Mr. Dink to place a pumpkin in the machine and set the dial to its scariest setting. Then, as the pumpkin carving machine started working, Doug asked his question. "Are vampires for real?" he inquired.

"Most scholars say that vampires are merely a superstition of ignorant people," Mr. Dink explained. "Why?"

"Everybody at school thinks Skeeter's a vampire," Doug admitted.

Mr. Dink looked curiously at Doug. "Now where would they get that idea?" he asked.

Before Doug could answer, the timer went off on the carving machine. Mr. Dink removed the jack-o-lantern.

"*AHHHHHHHH!*" Mr. Dink and Doug both screamed.

The jack-o-lantern looked just like Skeeter!

27

Chapter 7

The next morning, every kid at Beebe Bluff Middle School was talking about Skeeter.

"Skeeter's a bloody vampire," Chalky asserted.

"Not just a vampire," Skunky corrected him. "He's the Bat Master!"

"Skeeter Valentine sucks blood!" Roger announced.

But Doug still wouldn't believe it. "Skeeter can't be a vampire, guys," Doug insisted. "Where's the proof?"

"Let's look at the facts," Connie suggested. "Fact one: He's blue, the color of the Undead."

Most of the kids nodded. But Doug shook his head. What did being blue matter? In all of Doug's books about the legends of vampires he hadn't read anything about them being blue.

"And how could he be that smart—unless he was two hundred years old?" Roger added.

"He's got a, d'uh, bandage on his finger," Willy offered.

Doug looked curiously at Willy. "So what," he said. "He cut his finger."

"But vampires wrap themselves in bandages," Willy insisted.

"No they don't. That's mummies," Doug corrected him.

Willy's eyes bulged with fear. "You mean he's a mummy, too?!"

Roger didn't wait for a response. Instead he pulled a huge shopping bag from his locker. "I just bought the latest antivampire stuff to protect us from Valentine," he assured his pals as he pulled some garlic and a wooden stake from his bag.

Doug knew what they were for. Garlic was supposed to keep vampires away. And the only way to stop a vampire for good was to drive a wooden stake through his heart. *"Uck!"* he said.

Connie reached into Roger's bag. She pulled out a pair of glow-in-the-dark under-wear with Roger's face plastered all over them.

"How does this stop vampires?" Connie snickered. She held them up for everyone to see. The kids giggled.

Roger grabbed his new underpants and threw them back in the bag. "As long as I was shopping, I got some personalized underwear," he told the laughing crowd. Roger had a lot of money. And he used it to buy all sorts of expensive things, like jackets with temperature controls. Roger pulled a fancy video camera from the bottom of his bag. It was a spy camera. All Roger had to do was plant it in Skeeter's locker. He could operate it by remote control.

"This camera will show us what vampire stuff Valentine is hiding in his locker," Roger explained as he threaded the wires into Skeeter's locker.

Willy held up the video screen so everyone could see what was inside Skeeter's locker.

Doug didn't like this idea. A guy's locker was supposed to be private—like his pockets.

"Come on, Roger," Doug pleaded.

But Roger ignored Doug. He flicked on the camera. Suddenly everyone could see what was in Skeeter's locker. There were stickers, packs of gum, a pile of dirt. . . .

"Dirt!" Roger declared. "Probably the soil of his homeland so he can sleep in his locker."

"That's from his science experiment about dirt clods," Doug told him.

Then the camera shifted. It focused on a big white bag. The letters on the bag were unmistakable. They read BAT CHOW.

"Is that *Bat Chow*?" Doug gulped.

Roger nodded triumphantly. "Who's the clod now, Funnie?" he asked.

Doug kicked at the ground. There was no denying it. Skeeter was a vampire. Doug could just imagine him wolfing down the Bat Chow—*even making commercials for it!*

"Nothing goes with delicious Bat Chow like a cold frosty bottle of Vicious Bloodsucking Vampire Cola," Doug imagined

Skeeter saying on TV. Then he pictured Skeeter giving a fang-toothed smile and claiming, "I'd rather drink this than bite my best friend—right, Doug?"

In his imagination, Doug could see himself in a daze as a zombie slave, already bitten by Skeeter the Bat Master. "Yeeeesssss Masssterrrrrr," Doug would mumble.

It was a terrifying thought.

Doug blinked his eyes and shook his head, trying to erase the scene from his mind. "There has to be some explanation," Doug insisted.

"Yeah, your best friend's a bloodsucker," Roger sneered back.

Doug looked at his watch. Oh, no. Just when he thought things couldn't get any worse, it was time for band practice.

"I don't have time to argue," Doug said. "I've got to get to band practice." Doug picked up his banjo and left. Most of the other kids followed him. Only Roger and Willy stayed behind.

As Doug left for practice, Skeeter passed Roger and Willy in the hall.

"What're you doing, guys?" Skeeter asked innocently.

"*AAAAHHHHH!*" Willy and Roger took off screaming down the hall.

Skeeter watched them go. "What did I say?" he wondered aloud.

Chapter 8

Things were really getting strange at Beebe Bluff Middle School.

Kids all scrambled to find a place on the early bus. Doug got into line behind Connie and Roger. As usual, they were talking about vampires.

"Hey, I just realized Skeeter can't be a vampire," Doug told Connie and Roger. "Vampires have to sleep all day."

Roger snickered. "Those rules were probably made up by vampires to fool us," he said.

"Get on the bus, Doug," Connie added.

"Everybody in the whole school can't be wrong."

Doug took one last look at the bats in the tower. Then he boarded the bus behind Connie.

It seemed like Skeeter was the only person who hadn't heard that he was the Bat Master. At lunchtime the next day the whole cafeteria got quiet when he walked in the door. Everybody stared at him. They were frozen with fear.

"Hey guys," he greeted one table of kids. No one answered. Skeeter sat down next to Chalky and frowned. "Chalky, is everyone mad at me or something?" Skeeter asked.

Chalky covered his neck with his hands. "I dunno," he whispered nervously.

"Did you ever have the feeling someone is looking at you?" Skeeter remarked. Chalky shook his head and looked at the ground.

Roger was sitting just behind Skeeter,

watching his every move. "How would he know we were looking at him if he didn't have vampire powers?" Roger declared triumphantly.

That did it. Now everyone knew for sure that Skeeter was the Bat Master. Everyone sitting in the cafeteria got up and raced out the doors and into the hall in a giant stampede!

Skeeter was the only one left in the room.

Chapter 9

Doug went up to his room right after school. He was supposed to be working on his homework, but he was too busy reading a book about vampires.

Doug looked at the step-by-step pictures of a vampire turning into a bat. Was Skeeter doing that right now? he wondered. What did it feel like to be a vampire, anyway?

Doug closed the book and thought about it. Even if Skeeter was a vampire, he was still Skeeter. "So my best friend is a vampire," Doug told Porkchop. "Does that mean I can't be friends with him anymore?"

Doug tried to imagine Skeeter as a

vampire. They would still do the same things they always did. They could go to the amusement park and look in the fun-house mirrors—even if Skeeter couldn't see himself in the mirror because vampires don't have any reflection.

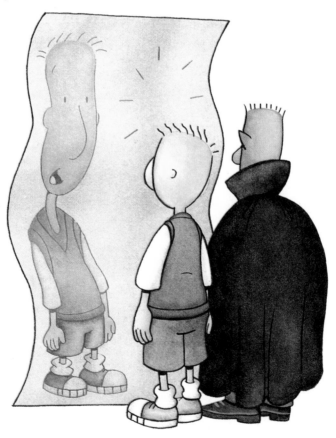

And Doug and Skeeter could still play Frisbee together. In fact, as a vampire, Skeeter could really come in handy when they played. If the Frisbee got caught in a tree, Skeeter could turn into a bat and fly up and get it.

Doug decided that having a friend who was a vampire could actually be pretty cool.

Unfortunately, Doug was the only one who felt that way. And at that very moment, the kids from school were all gathered at Doug's front door. They rang the bell. Doug went downstairs and let them inside.

"Funnie, we took a vote," Roger told Doug. "From now on, everybody stays clear of Skeeter Valentine."

"But why?" Doug asked. "What did Skeeter ever do to anybody?"

"He did this," Roger replied, thrusting a small white envelope in Doug's face.

"These are invitations to his house on Halloween, the scariest night of the year!" Roger exclaimed.

"So?" Doug asked.

"Don't you get it?" Beebe shouted at Doug. "He's caught on. He knows we know!"

Roger looked straight into Doug's eyes and said, "He wants to get us all together in one place and . . ." Doug watched as Roger pretended to chomp on Ned's neck. "Then he'll make us all zombie slaves of the Bat Master," Roger concluded.

Before Doug could respond, the phone

rang in the kitchen. Doug's mother picked it up and leaned out into the living room. "Skeeter's on the phone, Doug," she called.

Doug turned toward the kitchen. "Don't bite me!" Ned cried as he ran away from Doug.

"I'm not a vampire," Doug replied.

"Who else would be a vampire's friend?" Roger insisted.

The kids looked at Doug through new eyes. Then they ran to take cover behind his living room couch. Doug shivered. Now the gang thought *he* was a vampire, too!

"It's a question of public safety," Roger continued from his hiding spot behind a large chair. "If you talk to Valentine, nobody can talk to you."

"Prove to us you're not a vampire," Beebe taunted Doug.

Doug was standing by the front door, and he looked from the phone to the group of kids cowering nervously behind the couch. What was he going to do? What else *could* he do?

"Tell Skeeter I just stepped out," Doug called to his mother.

Roger came out from his hiding place and gave Doug a big thumbs-up.

Suddenly, Doug felt ill.

Chapter 10

On the night of Skeeter's party, Roger invited everyone to his house for an antivampire costume party. Roger dressed in fang-proof armor and decorated the room with garlic and wooden stakes. Just to be sure vampires couldn't get him, Roger even ate whole cloves of garlic. P. U.! He wanted to be safe, inside and out!

All of the kids except Skeeter were at the party. Doug felt bad about not going to Skeeter's party, but he tried not to let the other kids know. He didn't want to risk being called a vampire again.

Roger passed a plate of garlic cloves

around the room. "Want some garlic, Funnie?" he asked Doug.

Doug held his nose and shook his head. "No, thanks."

Roger put his arm around Doug. Doug turned his head. Roger's breath was really stinky! "I'm glad you came, Dougie-boy," Roger said. "It's nice to know we're *all* safe from vampires."

Doug breathed a sigh of relief as Roger walked away. Then he walked over to Patti. "Do you think I should at least call Skeeter?" Doug asked her. He was starting to feel guilty about abandoning his best friend on Halloween.

"I don't know," Patti answered honestly. "This vampire thing is really getting out of hand."

While Doug and the rest of the gang were busy avoiding Roger's garlic breath, Skeeter was sitting alone in his basement. His father came downstairs and put his arm around him. "Wasn't your party tonight?" Mr.

Valentine asked gently. "Where are the people, you know, the people who like you?"

"You mean friends?" Skeeter asked. "I don't have any. Nobody likes me anymore. I thought if I had a party, at least they would come. Even Doug didn't show up. And he's my best friend. At least I *thought* he was."

Skeeter sighed. He was having the worst Halloween ever.

* * *

Doug's Halloween wasn't going much better. While the other kids were playing "pin the stake on the vampire," Doug was busy trying to imagine life without Skeeter as his best friend. He imagined himself playing Ping Pong all by himself. That wouldn't be much fun—there'd be no one there to hit the ball back to him. Then Doug imagined himself all alone in one of those shopping mall photo booths. That wouldn't work, either. Doug would feel pretty stupid making faces for the camera all by himself.

Even imagining wasn't any fun without Skeeter! "I can't dump my best friend!" Doug said aloud.

Connie was shocked. "Is a friendship worth dying for?" she asked.

But Doug wasn't convinced that Skeeter was a vampire. "Connie, your rumor about talking gerbils in the science lab was wrong," Doug confronted her. "Maybe you're wrong about Skeeter, too."

Connie stood her ground. "There's too much proof," she insisted. "You saw him with the bats."

"I did, too," Skunky added.

"And he's really weird," Beebe suggested.

"That doesn't make him a monster," Doug insisted. "Maybe some people think you're weird, too, Beebe."

Beebe glared at Doug. "Oh, come on. Who could think I'm weird?"

Some kids looked away. Others started to whistle. Obviously a lot of people did think Beebe was weird.

"But he's having a party," Roger insisted. "He's never had a party before."

Doug looked around the room. It seemed like it was all the kids against him. Still, Doug wasn't giving up on Skeeter—even if he *was* the only one on Skeeter's side.

Patti walked over and stood beside Doug. "Maybe Skeeter is having a party because everyone's been avoiding him and he feels lonely," she suggested.

49

Some of the kids nodded. That sounded pretty reasonable to them—until Roger opened his mouth, that is.

"You're forgetting one thing," Roger said. "HE'S A *VAMPIRE!*"

"Yeah, that's right," the other kids agreed.

Doug headed for the door. "The least we can do is ask Skeeter about it," Doug said. "Anybody with me?"

Nobody was. So Doug left the party alone.

Roger watched nervously as Doug slammed the door behind him. He had a horrible thought. "If Funnie gets bitten, then he'll bite some of us, and pretty soon we'll *all* be vampires!" Roger declared. "And if we're *all* vampires, who do *we* get to bite? Either way, we're jinxed."

Now the kids would have *two* vampires to worry about!

The gang dashed out the door and raced down the block. They had to stop Doug Funnie from becoming a vampire!

Chapter II

Doug hadn't even reached Skeeter's house when he saw the other kids catching up to him. Doug thought they were *all* going to Skeeter's party.

Wow! I convinced them! Doug thought proudly. They're coming to Skeeter's after all!

But as the mob got closer, Doug heard his friends screaming. "There he is!" Roger shouted. "Get him! Stop Funnie!"

The angry mob charged at Doug. "Uh-oh," Doug cried out. He made a quick turn through the playground, hopped over a fence, and hid behind a tree. But no matter where he went, the gang of kids was always close behind.

Finally, Doug reached Skeeter's house. He raced down to the basement. He found Skeeter sitting all alone, dressed as a vampire.

"Hey, Doug," Skeeter mumbled sadly.

Doug had to act fast. He could hear the other kids' footsteps coming up the walk to Skeeter's house.

"Skeet, everyone says you're a vampire, and they . . ."

Doug never got to finish his sentence. The gang of kids, led by Roger and Connie, burst through the basement door and came stomping down the stairs. Roger took one look at Skeeter's vampire costume and grinned triumphantly.

"Joey Cucamunga!" he declared, "I knew it!" Roger made a big **X** with his fingers. Then he shoved his crossed fingers in Skeeter's face. "Melt, vampire, melt!" he ordered.

But Skeeter didn't melt. Instead he went over and flicked off the lights. The room went dark! Giant bats dropped from the ceiling and sprang from the walls! Everybody began screaming!

"Cool surprise, huh?" Skeeter asked. "I made them myself."

"Don't bite me. Bite them!" Roger cried out in fear.

Doug felt one of the bats. It was rubber—just a model bat on a spring.

Patti also knew the bats weren't real. "The bats are fake," she told everyone. Then she turned and smiled at Skeeter. "You're not a vampire, are you?" she asked him.

Skeeter stood proud and tall. "You thought I was a vampire?" he asked. "Wow! Is my costume that good?"

Connie looked sheepishly at the ground. "No. It's because of my big mouth. I started a stupid rumor," she admitted.

But Skunky wasn't convinced. There were still some unanswered questions. "Hold it," he demanded. "Why were you up there with the bats?"

"Because Mr. Crushie is afraid of bats," Skeeter explained. "So, for a science project, I helped them find a new home."

Skeeter explained that he used Bat Chow to lure the bats into a specially made bat carrier. Then he carried the bats into the park and set them free.

"I figured they would like the park—there are lots of nice trees to hang in," Skeeter said, finishing his story.

"So that's why you had Bat Chow in your locker," Doug said. "It all makes sense now."

Roger stood up and smiled nervously. "So, how'd you like my performance, suckers?" he asked. "This was my Halloween costume—the scared guy."

Doug shook his head. Roger would never apologize. Some things never changed.

Skeeter went over to the stereo and popped in a tape. Everyone started dancing, singing, and bobbing for apples. Skeeter's bash was the best Halloween party ever!

"I can't believe we almost missed Skeeter's great party because of a stupid rumor," Doug said as he popped a bat-shaped cookie in his mouth.

Doug knew better now. Just because somebody says something's true, that doesn't make it true.

GET A FREE ISSUE OF

The fun-filled magazine that kids enjoy and parents applaud.

A whopping one million kids ages 7 to 14 are dedicated to reading **Disney Adventures**—you will be, too!

Each month DA plugs kids into supercharged fun . . .

- **The inside scoop on movie stars and athletes**
- **Hot new video games and how to beat 'em**
- **The characters kids love**
- **Stories about everyday kids**
- ***PLUS:*** **puzzles, contests, trivia, comics, and much, much more!**

- -

Now on home video, Doug's Vampire Caper!

Is there really a Bat Master skulking around the halls of the school?

Are there bats in the school's clock tower?

Catch Doug, Skeeter, Connie, and the mysterious Bat Master as they come to full-color life in this new animated cartoon.

Do you dig

BRAND SPANKING NEW!

DOUG?

Read all of the Doug books!

Doug's Big Shoe Disaster
ISBN 0-7868-3142-1
$8.95 ($11.95 CAN)

Doug's Secret Christmas
ISBN 0-7868-3155-3
$8.95 ($11.95 CAN)

Doug's Hoop Nightmare
ISBN 0-7868-4151-6
$3.50 ($4.95 CAN)

Doug's Big Comeback
ISBN 0-7868-4150-8
$3.50 ($4.95 CAN)

Doug's Journal
ISBN 0-7868-4154-0
$6.95 ($9.95 CAN)

Available at your local bookstore.